W9-CON-881

First U.S. small hardcover edition 2005

Library of Congress
Cataloging-in-Publication Data
is available.

Library of Congress Catalog
Card Number 97-024146

ISBN 0-7636-0312-0 (large hardcover)
ISBN 0-7636-2700-3 (small hardcover)

2 4 6 8 10 9 7 5 3 1

Printed in China

This book was typeset in Wallyfont.

Candlewick Press
2067 Massachusetts Avenue
Cambridge, Massachusetts
02140

visit us at
www.candlewick.com

WHERE'S WALDO?

THE WONDER BOOK

MARTIN HANDFORD

CANDLEWICK PRESS
CAMBRIDGE, MASSACHUSETTS

ONCE UPON A PAGE...

HEY, WALDO FANS! LOOK AT ALL THESE BRILLIANT BOOKS! LOOK AT ALL THE CHARACTERS WHO HAVE STEPPED OUT FROM THEIR PAGES! WOW! WHAT A MAGIC SCENE! THESE BOOKS HAVE REALLY COME ALIVE — THAT BOOK OVER THERE IS ABOUT MY TRAVELS! AND WOOF, WENDA, WIZARD WHITEBEARD, AND ODLAW ALL HAVE SPECIAL BOOKS OF THEIR OWN. NOW YOU CAN JOIN US TOO, IF YOU CAN FIND US, AND WE'LL TRAVEL TOGETHER THROUGH ALL THE OTHER WONDERFUL SCENES IN THIS WONDER BOOK. ONE SCENE IS MY SPECIAL FAVORITE — YOU'LL NEVER GUESS WHAT MAKES IT SO GREAT. THE BOOKMARK MARKS IT, SO WHEN WE GET THERE, YOU WILL KNOW. NOW GET SEARCHING, WALDO-FOLLOWERS, AND OFF WE GO! AND BE PREPARED FOR LOTS OF SURPRISES ALONG THE WAY!

Waldo

THE SEARCH IS ON! FIND THESE FIVE INTREPID TRAVELERS IN EVERY SCENE IN THE WONDER BOOK!

- FIND WALDO . . . WHO TRAVELS EVERYWHERE!
- FIND WOOF . . . WHO WAGS HIS TAIL!
  (WHICH IS ALL YOU CAN SEE!)
- FIND WENDA . . . WHO TAKES THE PICTURES!
- FIND WIZARD WHITEBEARD . . . WHO CASTS THE SPELLS!
- FIND ODLAW . . . WHOSE GOOD DEEDS ARE FEW INDEED!

THE SEARCH CONTINUES! NEXT FIND THESE IMPORTANT THINGS THE TRAVELERS HAVE LOST!

FIND WALDO'S LOST KEY!
FIND WOOF'S LOST BONE!
FIND WENDA'S LOST CAMERA!
FIND WIZARD WHITEBEARD'S MAGIC SCROLL!
FIND ODLAW'S LOST BINOCULARS!

THE GAME OF GAMES

FOUR HUGE TEAMS ARE PLAYING THIS GREAT GAME OF GAMES. THE REFEREES ARE TRYING TO SEE THAT NO ONE BREAKS THE RULES. BETWEEN THE STARTING LINE AT THE TOP AND THE FINISH LINE AT THE BOTTOM, THERE ARE LOTS OF PUZZLES, BOOBY TRAPS, AND TESTS. THE GREEN TEAMS NEARLY WON, AND THE ORANGE TEAMS HARDLY STARTED! CAN YOU SPOT THE ONLY ORANGE TEAM PLAYER WHO HAS FINISHED? AND THE ONLY GREEN TEAM PLAYER WHO HAS NOT YET BEGUN?

5+4=9

2+2=7

TOYS! TOYS! TOYS!

WOW! ALL THE TEENY-TINY TOY CREATURES ARE COMING OUT OF THE TOY BOX TO EXPLORE THE PLAYROOM! THE BOOKS ARE TOO HUGE TO READ BUT THE GREEN ONE IS PERFECT AS A SOCCER FIELD! SWOOSH! AND THE BOOKMARK MAKES A GREAT SLIDE! CAN YOU SEE A TEDDY TAKING OFF IN A PAPER PLANE? AND A DINOSAUR

CHASING A CAVEMAN? WHAT HIGH JINKS AND HIGH-WIRE ACTS ARE HAPPENING HERE! SO DO YOU THINK THAT THE TOYS ALWAYS HAVE GREAT TIMES LIKE THESE WHEN NO ONE IS AROUND?

BRIGHT LIGHTS AND NIGHT FRIGHTS

HEY! WHAT BLAZING BEAMS OF LIGHT, WHAT A DAZZLING DISPLAY! GLITTER, TWINKLE, SPARKLE, FLASH — LOOK HOW BRIGHTLY THESE LIGHTHOUSES LIGHT UP THE NIGHT! BUT, OH NO, THE MONSTERS WANT TO PUT THE LIGHTS OUT! THEY'RE ATTACKING FROM ALL SIDES. THE SAILORS ARE SQUIRTING PINK GOO AT THEM, BUT THE MONSTERS SPURT GREEN GOO RIGHT BACK! BUT WAIT! THREE OF THE MONSTERS ARE FIRING DIFFERENT COLORED GOO! SPLASH, SPLAT, SPLURGE! CAN YOU SEE THEM, WALDO-WATCHERS?

THE CAKE FACTORY

Mmmm! FEAST YOUR EYES, WALDO-WATCHERS! SNIFF THE DELICIOUS SMELLS OF BAKING CAKES! DROOL AT THE TASTY TOPPINGS! CAN YOU SEE A CAKE LIKE A TEAPOT, A CAKE LIKE A HOUSE, A CAKE SO TALL A WORKER ON THE FLOOR ABOVE IS LICKING IT? CAKES, CAKES, EVERYWHERE! HOW SCRUMPTIOUS! HOW YUM-YUM-YUMPTIOUS! LOOK

AT THE OOZING SUGAR ICING AND THE SHINY RED CHERRIES ON THE ROOF UP THERE! THAT ROOM IS WHERE THE FACTORY CONTROLLERS WORK, BUT HAVE THEY LOST CONTROL?

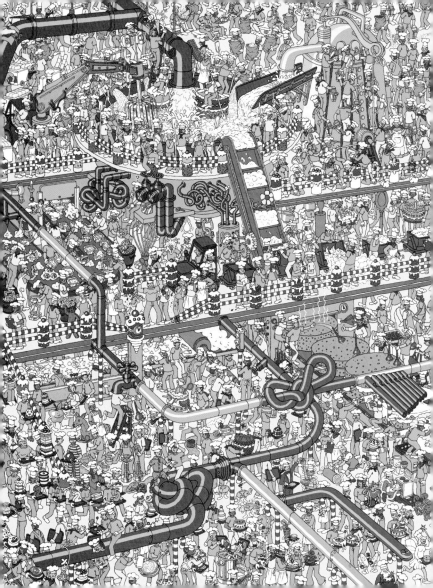

THE ODLAW SWAMP

THE BRAVE ARMY OF MANY HATS IS TRYING TO GET THROUGH THIS FEARFUL SWAMP. HUNDREDS OF ODLAWS AND BLACK-AND-YELLOW SWAMP CREATURES ARE CAUSING TROUBLE IN THE UNDERGROWTH. THE REAL ODLAW IS THE ONE CLOSEST TO HIS LOST PAIR OF BINOCULARS. CAN YOU FIND HIM, X-RAY-EYED ONES? HOW MANY DIFFERENT KINDS OF HATS CAN YOU SEE ON THE SOLDIERS' HEADS? SQUELCH! SQUELCH! I'M GLAD I'M NOT IN THEIR SHOES! ESPECIALLY AS THEIR FEET ARE IN THE MURKY MUD!

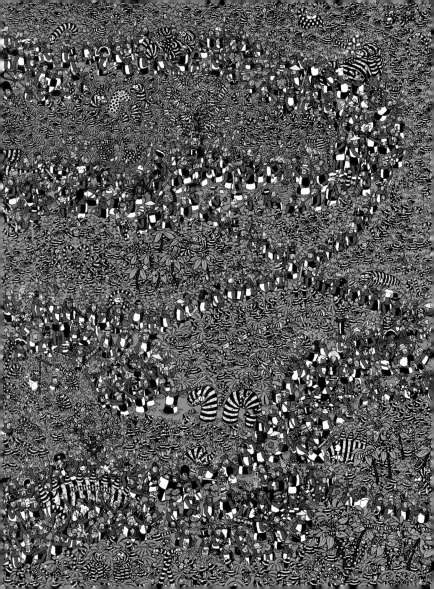

CLOWN TOWN

Clap your feet, Waldo-jokers! Stamp your hands! You'll go oogly-boogly-woogly-eyed with wonder! Here are hundreds of clowns playing pranks and making mischief! Look at their colorful costumes — with fluffy pom-poms galore! And their bright and shiny noses! Toot, toot! Can you see a car with its tongue sticking out?

Ting-a-ling! And a bike with square wheels? Tee-hee! Ha-ha! What happiness it is to be in Clown Town! Splash! Splat! Except for all those squirty flowers and custard pies!

THE FANTASTIC FLOWER GARDEN

WOW! WHAT A BRIGHT AND DAZZLING GARDEN SPECTACLE! ALL THE FLOWERS ARE IN FULL BLOOM, AND HUNDREDS OF BUSY GARDENERS ARE WATERING AND TENDING THEM. THE PETAL COSTUMES THEY ARE WEARING MAKE THEM LOOK LIKE FLOWERS THEMSELVES! VEGETABLES ARE GROWING IN THE GARDEN TOO. HOW MANY DIFFERENT KINDS

CAN YOU SEE? SNIFF THE AIR, WALDO-FOLLOWERS! SMELL THE FANTASTIC SCENTS! WHAT A TREAT FOR YOUR NOSES AS WELL AS YOUR EYES!

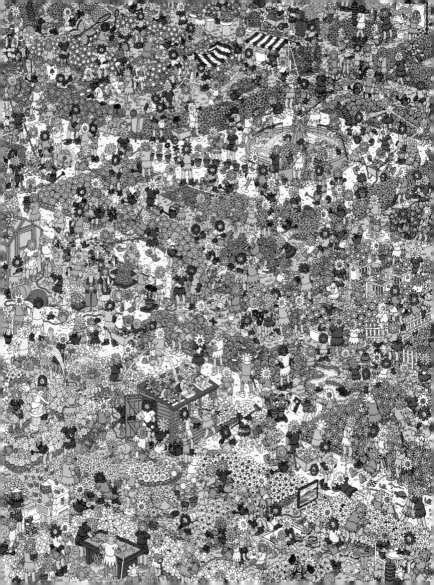

THE CORRIDORS OF TIME

TICK-TOCK, TICK-TOCK! THE HANDS OF ALL THE CLOCKS EXCEPT ONE SAY A QUARTER TO TWELVE. WHAT A DING-DONG THERE WILL BE WHEN THEY STRIKE! CAN YOU FIND THE ONLY CLOCK THAT TELLS A DIFFERENT TIME? IN THIS SCENE ARE THIRTY-SEVEN DOORS. ABOVE EACH DOOR APPEARS THE SHAPE OF THE KEY THAT WILL UNLOCK IT. CAN YOU FIND THE KEYS IN THE CROWD BRAINY ONES, AND MATCH THEM TO THE SHAPES? OH, NO! ONE DOOR HAS NO SHAPE ABOVE IT! EVEN SO YOU MUST FIND ITS KEY!

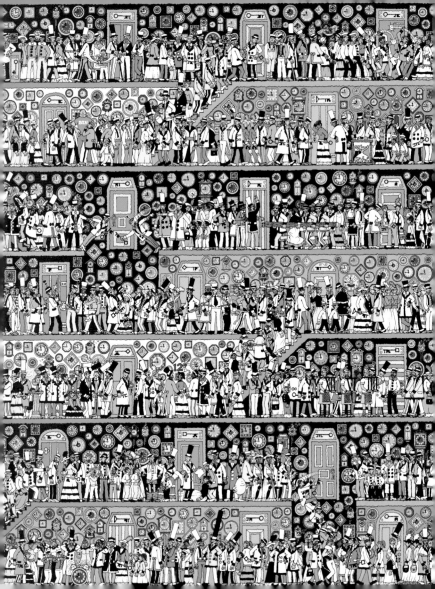

THE LAND OF WOOFS

HEY! LOOK AT ALL THESE DOGS THAT ARE DRESSED LIKE WOOF! BOW WOW WOW! IN THIS LAND A DOG'S LIFE IS THE HIGHLIFE! THERE'S A LUXURY WOOF HOTEL WITH A BONE-SHAPED SWIMMING POOL, AND AT THE WOOF RACETRACK, LOTS OF WOOFS ARE CHASING ATTENDANTS DRESSED AS CATS, SAUSAGES, AND POSTMEN! THE BOOKMARK IS ON THIS PAGE, WALDO-FOLLOWERS. SO NOW YOU KNOW, THIS IS MY FAVORITE SCENE! THIS IS THE ONLY SCENE IN THE BOOK WHERE YOU CAN SEE MORE OF THE REAL WOOF THAN JUST HIS TAIL! BUT CAN YOU FIND HIM? HE'S THE ONLY ONE WITH FIVE RED STRIPES ON HIS TAIL! HERE'S ANOTHER CHALLENGE! ELEVEN

TRAVELERS HAVE FOLLOWED ME HERE — ONE FROM EVERY SCENE. CAN YOU SEE THEM? AND CAN YOU FIND WHERE EACH ONE JOINED ME ON MY ADVENTURES, AND SPOT ALL THEIR APPEARANCES AFTERWARDS! KEEP ON SEARCHING, WALDO FANS! HAVE A WONDERFUL, WONDERFUL TIME!

THE GREAT
WHERE'S WALDO?
THE WONDER BOOK
CHECKLIST

More and more wonderful things
for Waldo fans to check out!

ONCE UPON A PAGE...

- Helen of Troy and Paris
- Rudyard Kipling and the jungle book
- Sir Francis and his drake
- Wild Bill hiccup
- A shopping centaur
- Handel's water music
- George washing ton
- Samuel peeps at his diary
- Guy forks
- Tchaikovsky and the nut cracker sweet
- A Roundhead with a round head
- Pythagoras and the square of the hippopotamus
- William shakes spear
- Madame two swords
- Garibaldi and his biscuits
- Florence and her nightingale
- The pilgrim fathers
- Captain cook
- Hamlet making an omelet
- Jason and the juggernauts
- Whistling Whistler painting his mother
- Ali barber
- Lincoln and the Gettysburg address
- Billy the kid
- Two knights fighting the war of the roses
- The Duke of Wellington's wellington

THE MIGHTY FRUIT FIGHT

- A box of dates next to a box of dates
- "A pair of date palms
- An apple a day keeps the doctor away?"
- Six crab apples
- Four naval oranges
- Blueberries wearing blue berets
- A kiwi fruit
- A banana doing the splits
- A pine apple
- Three fruit fools
- A bowl of fruit and a can of fruit
- Cranberry saws
- An orange upsetting the apple cart
- A banana tree
- Cooking apples
- Elder berry wine
- Seven wild cherries
- Goose berries
- A partridge in a pear tree
- A fruit cock's tail
- Two peach halves
- "The Big Apple"
- One sour apple without a beg
- Paw paw fruit
- Another apple cart being

THE ODLAW SWAMP

- Two soldiers disguised as Odlaws
- A soldier wearing a bowler hat
- A soldier wearing a stovepipe hat
- A soldier wearing a riding helmet
- A soldier wearing a straw hat
- Three soldiers wearing peaked caps
- A lady wearing an Easter bonnet
- Two soldiers wearing football helmets
- Two soldiers wearing baseball caps
- A big shield next to a little shield
- A lady wearing a sun hat
- A soldier with two big feathers in his hat
- Some rattle snakes
- Five romantic snakes
- Seven wooden tots
- Three small wooden boats
- Four birds' nests
- One Odlaw in disguise
- A swamp creature without stripes
- A monster cleaning its teeth
- A monster asleep, but not for long
- A soldier floating on a package
- A very big monster with a very small head
- One charmed snake
- Five charmed spears
- A snake resting

CLOWN TOWN

- A clown reading a newspaper
- A starry umbrella
- A clown with a blue teapot
- Two hoses leaking
- A clown with two hoops on each arm
- A clown looking through a telescope
- Two clowns holding big hammers
- A clown with a bag of party favors
- Two clowns swinging flowerpots
- A clown combing the roof of a Clown Town house
- Six flowers spilling out of a balloon
- A clown squirting the water clown
- A clown wearing a jack-in-the-box hat
- Three cars
- A clown with a fishing rod
- One hat joining two clowns
- A clown about to catapult a custard pie
- Clowns wearing tea shirts
- Three clowns with buckets of water
- A clown with a yo-yo
- A clown slipping into a custard pie
- Seventeen clouds
- A clown having his foot tickled
- One clown with a green nose

THE FANTASTIC FLOWER GARDEN

- The yellow rose of Texas
- Flower pots and flower beds
- Butter flies
- Gardeners sowing seeds and planting bulbs
- A garden nursery
- A bird bath and a bird table
- House plants, wall flowers, and blue bells
- Cabbage patches, tiger lilies, and fox gloves
- A hedgehog, next to a hedge hog
- A flower border and a flower show
- A bull frog
- Earth worms
- A wheelbarrow full of wheels
- A cricket match
- Parsley, sage, Rosemary, and time
- A queen bee near a honey comb
- A landscape gardener
- A sun dial next to a sundial
- Gardeners dancing to the beetles
- A green house and a tree house
- A spring onion and a leek with a leak
- Door mice
- An apple tree
- Weeping willows and climbing roses
- Rock pool

THE CORRIDORS OF

- The clock striking twelve
- Clock faces
- Wall clocks
- An egg timer
- A clock tower
- A very loud alarm clock
- A traveling clock
- A runner racing against time
- Roman numerals
- Time flies
- An hour glass
- Big Ben
- Old Father Time
- Grandfather clocks
- A walking stick
- Thirty six pairs of almost identical twins
- One pair of identical twins
- A man's suspenders being pulled in opposite directions
- A swinging pendulum
- Coattails tied in a knot
- A door and half log hat
- A very tall top hat
- A pair of hooked umbrellas
- A sundial
- A clock cuckoo
- A pair of tangled walking sticks

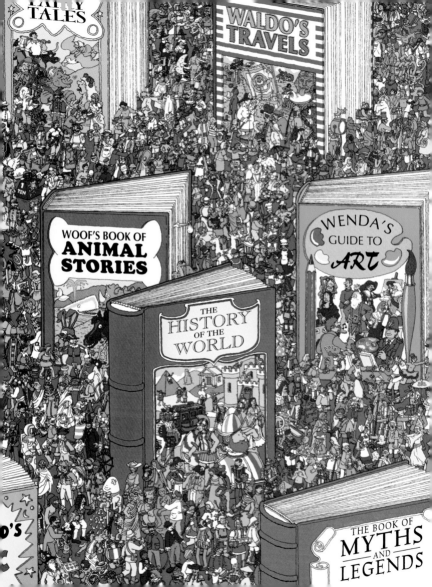